D1294422

34170083950767

The Peace Tree
from *Hiroshima*

The Little Bonsai with a Big Story

Sandra Moore
illustrations by Kazumi Wilds

TUTTLE Publishing

Tokyo | Rutland, Vermont | Singapore

I was born nearly four hundred years ago on the island of Miyajima. As I pushed up through the dirt, I saw my reflection in the mountain lake. A forest of tall trees surrounded me: cedar, greenwillow, and hinoki. Macaques, momongas, and bats darted between their leaves and limbs.

One morning, as the summer sun beat down, I saw a man. Alone, with a basket strapped to his back, he spoke to the beautiful trees. Later I would learn his name: Itaro.

"I must bring back a souvenir of this island, of the trees that touched my heart," said Itaro. Then he did something that changed my life forever.

He carefully dug around my roots, gently picked up my small pine branches, and wrapped me in a cloth, wet from a nearby stream. Soon, I was his companion on the mountain trail, leaving the forest behind.

Itaro's house seemed strangely
quiet at first. I missed the gentle rain
on my branches and the monkeys
squawking high in the leaf canopy. But I
grew to like my new home and the ceramic
pot in which I was planted. For over fifty years
Itaro watered me and pruned my branches, shaping
me like a sculptor into a miniature bonsai tree.

"You remind me of the magical island I visited," said Itaro, his hair now white with age. "That's why I called you Miyajima."

7

When Itaro died, his son Wajiro looked after me.
And when Wajiro needed a cane to help him walk,
he taught his son Somegoro how to care for me.

8

For three hundred years, the job of watching over me was passed down from father to son.

9

When our family moved to Hiroshima, it was
Masaru who looked after me. He added more
bonsai to our household. Beech, black pine,
and blue juniper trees joined me on the porch.

In 1945, something terrible happened. A war raged in Asia, and Hiroshima was hit by an atomic bomb. It exploded two miles from my house.

Many, many people were hurt or killed, and most buildings were reduced to rubble.

Our family was fortunate. Though our windows were shattered, we were injured only a little by the flying glass. Masaru dropped to his knees and bowed, as a sign of gratitude. I, too, felt like bowing, as my friend was unharmed.

For several years, everyone in Hiroshima suffered
terribly. But slowly, Masaru returned to his
daily bonsai care: watering and pruning,
wiring and shaping. And as we revived,
his heavy heart became lighter.

15

And slowly the people began to rebuild. In ten years, our city had new streets, sidewalks, and spirit. Just miles from our porch, the Peace Memorial Park opened its gates.

Twenty years later, the classrooms were once again teeming
with children, and the fields were full of cosmos flowers.

Then, thirty years after the war, my life took the most
surprising turn of all.

A brilliant yellow sun rose over Hiroshima one morning as Masaru joined our tree family on the porch.

"America is having a special celebration, for its two-hundredth birthday. The Japanese people will send a collection of bonsai trees as a gift. I have thought long and hard about how I could part with any of my beloved *kodomotachi*—my children."

He closed his eyes and took in a long, slow breath.

"Miyajima, you have seen the sadness created by war between Japan and America. You have felt the hope that helped us to rebuild. You are stronger than ever, and patient, and wise. I hope you will understand if I ask you, my favorite white pine, to become a tree of peace."

When the truck arrived to take me to the airport in Tokyo, Masaru's grandson, Akira, shouted "I'll miss you, Miyajima!" as he waved goodbye.

A few days later, I arrived in America. At the National Arboretum in Washington, I joined a new bonsai family.

I heard the tour guide say, "This tree
survived the war between our country and
Japan and is now called the Peace Tree."

I felt very proud.

23

The next year, our arboretum had a special visitor. He arrived from the airport in a long, black limousine. As he surveyed the bonsai collection, my heart stopped. It was Masaru.

He looked old and frail. He was holding the hand of a young Japanese boy I recognized. It was his grandson, Akira.

"Akira is in America for the first time to visit you, Miyajima," he said. "It's important for us to see that you are well cared for. You are a special tree. A sign of peace between our country and the United States."

"You look happy here, Miyajima," said Akira,
reaching out to touch the bark on my trunk.
"Next spring," he said, "We will come again."

27

JAPANESE WHITE PINE

Miyajima

In training since 1625.

A gift of Masaru Yamaki and
his family.

Author's Note

This book is based on a true story. In 1976, the Japanese people gave the United States fifty bonsai trees (one for each of America's fifty states) as a present for America's Bicentennial, or two-hundredth-birthday celebration. The Emperor of Japan also added three trees from his private collection. Masaru Yamaki donated his family's beloved bonsai tree to the National Arboretum in Washington, D.C.

I've nicknamed the bonsai in this story Miyajima, after the island where it was born, during the time of castles and samurai. At the National Arboretum the bonsai is referred to as the "Yamaki pine" in honor of the Japanese family that cared for it for over three hundred years, and also as "the Peace Tree" because it is a symbol of friendship between Japan and America, two countries that were enemies during the Second World War.

In 1979, Masaru Yamaki flew to Washington to tour the bonsai collection. He stopped to look most carefully at the white pine his family had donated. When his host saw that Masaru had tears in his eyes, he asked, "Is everything okay?"

"Oh yes," replied Masaru, "These are tears of joy, because I can tell the tree is happy here."

While it's true that Masaru had two grandsons, in real life they didn't go with him to America. But when they were college students, Akira and Shigeru Yamaki visited the United States to meet the little bonsai tree—the oldest member of their family. When they returned to Japan, their grandfather told them the white pine had survived the bombing of Hiroshima. Masaru died a few years before I wrote this story, but Shigeru told me he felt his grandfather would "rejoice in the heavens" to know that his little bonsai's big story would be shared with others.

Glossary

arboretum A kind of outdoor museum where trees, shrubs, herbs, and flowers are studied by scientists and enjoyed by visitors. The National Arboretum in Washington, D.C. is home to a bonsai museum called The National Bonsai and Penjing Museum. The "Yamaki pine" (Miyajima) at the heart of this story is the oldest bonsai in the arboretum's collection.

bonsai (BONE-sigh) In Japanese *bon* means "shallow tray" or "pot," and *sai* means "plant." So the phrase "tree in a pot" is often used instead of the word "bonsai."

Hiroshima (He-ROH-shi-ma) A Japanese city on the island of Honshu. Honshu is the largest of many islands that make up the country of Japan. Hiroshima is best known because it was the first city in history to be hit by an atomic bomb.

kodomotachi (ko-DO-mo-ta-chee) The Japanese word for "children." In this story, Masaru uses the word to refer to his bonsai trees, whom he considered to be a part of his family.

macaque (ma-KACK) One of the most common types of monkeys in the world. The Japanese macaque has brown-grey fur, a red face, and a short tail. Japanese macaques are also called snow monkeys because they usually live in places where snow covers the ground for much of the year.

Miyajima (Mee-yah-JEAM-ah) A Japanese island (depicted on the endpapers of this book) that is known for its scenic beauty. It is sometimes referred to as the "Island of the Gods."

momonga (mo-MON-ga) A dwarf flying squirrel that lives in the mountain forests of Japan. Its back is grey and brown, its stomach is white, and it has a wide, flattened tail. Momongas are nocturnal.

Facts about Bonsai

Bonsai is an ancient art. Bonsai originated in China, and has been practiced in Japan for more than a thousand years. Unlike artists who use paint or clay to create works of art, the bonsai artist begins with a seedling or very small tree and shapes it with special tools over the course of many years.

Bonsai exist in many forms. Bonsai can be a single tree, a forest grouping of several trees, or even a miniature landscape, such as a mountainside

complete with rocks and bushes. One of the best-known bonsai, called Goshin (bottom of facing page), actually holds eleven small trees. Bonsai artist John Naka began with one tree in the pot and added more as his family grew. In the end, there was one tree to represent each of his eleven grandchildren.

Bonsai can be trained. Bonsai artists train their trees using tools like pruning shears, but some of the most dramatic effects result from their manipulating the trunk or branches of a tree with wire to create beautiful, snakelike curves.

Most bonsai are pretty small. Bonsai trees usually range in height from six inches to two feet. Many of the bonsai in the National Arboretum's collection could fit on your school desk. Miyajima, the bonsai in this story, which has had many centuries to grow, is three and a half feet tall—about the height of a six-year-old child.

Some bonsai are really tiny. One style of bonsai, known as *shito*, is small enough to be grown in thimble-sized pot—but this style is quite rare.

Bonsai leaves are smaller than regular leaves. The leaves of certain bonsai, like a Japanese maple, change colors in the fall and drop to the ground like a full-sized maple tree you might find in a yard or forest. However, the leaves are usually much tinier than those on a full-sized tree. If you had a toy rake, you could make a pile of miniature leaves for a doll to jump in.

Bonsai fruit is bigger than you'd think. If a bonsai is created from a fruit-bearing tree like an apple or lemon tree, the fruit is much larger than you would expect from such a small tree.

Bonsai can live for a long time. One of the longest-lived bonsai ever, a nine-hundred-year-old Japanese tree named Fudo, was purchased by the Brooklyn Botanical Garden in 1969. Unfortunately the tree did not adapt well to its new home, and died soon afterwards.

ALL PHOTOS COURTESY U.S. NATIONAL ARBORETUM

Acknowledgments

Sandra Moore would like to thank Johann Klodzen and Felix Laughlin of the National Bonsai Foundation for being so generous with their time and knowledge, as well as Yasuo, Shigeru, and Akira Yamaki for sharing the history of their beloved bonsai and giving her permission to turn it into a story for children. She would also like to thank her writing mentor, Mary Quattlebaum, and her husband, Mark Felsenthal, for his endless patience and support.

Kazumi Wilds would like to thank Jack Sustic of the National Bonsai and Penjing Museum at the U.S. National Arboretum for sharing his wisdom about bonsai and the special history of the Yamaki pine. She would also like to thank BJ & Gary DeBusschere, and Mehdi Kashkooli who provided a comfortable environment in which to illustrate this book, and her son Hajime, who waited patiently while she worked.

Published by Tuttle Publishing, an imprint of
Periplus Editions (HK) Ltd.

www.tuttlepublishing.com

Copyright © 2015 by Periplus Editions (HK) Ltd.

All rights reserved. No part of this publication may be reproduced or utilized in any form or by any means, electronic or mechanical, including photocopying, recording, or by any information storage and retrieval system, without prior written permission from the publisher.

Library of Congress Cataloging-in-Publication Data

Moore, Sandra, 1955-
 The peace tree from Hiroshima : a little Japanese bonsai with a big story / by Sandra Moore ; illustrated by Kazumi Wilds. -- First edition.
    pages cm
 Summary: A fictionalized account of a bonsai tree that lived with the Yamaki family in Hiroshima, Japan, for more than 300 years before being donated to the National Arboretum in Washington, D.C., in 1976 as a gesture of friendship and peace to celebrate the American Bicentennial.
 ISBN 978-4-8053-1347-3 (hardback) -- ISBN 978-1-4629-1723-5 (ebook) [1. Bonsai--Fiction. 2. Trees--Fiction. 3. Japan--History--1912-1945--Fiction. 4. Japan--History--1945-1989--Fiction. 5. Japan--Relations--United States--Fiction. 6. United States--Relations--Japan--Fiction.] I. Wilds, Kazumi, illustrator. II. Title.
 PZ7.1.M664Pe 2015
 [E]--dc23
                          2015017392

ISBN 978-4-8053-1347-3

Distributed by

North America, Latin America & Europe
Tuttle Publishing
364 Innovation Drive, North Clarendon, VT 05759-9436 U.S.A.
Tel: (802) 773-8930; Fax: (802) 773-6993
info@tuttlepublishing.com; www.tuttlepublishing.com

Japan
Tuttle Publishing
Yaekari Building, 3rd Floor, 5-4-12 Osaki, Shinagawa-ku, Tokyo 141 0032
Tel: (81) 3 5437-0171; Fax: (81) 3 5437-0755
sales@tuttle.co.jp; www.tuttle.co.jp

Asia Pacific
Berkeley Books Pte. Ltd.
61 Tai Seng Avenue #02-12, Singapore 534167
Tel: (65) 6280-1330; Fax: (65) 6280-6290
inquiries@periplus.com.sg; www.periplus.com

First edition
18 17 16 15   10 9 8 7 6 5 4 3 2   1510TW
Printed in Malaysia

TUTTLE PUBLISHING® is a registered trademark of Tuttle Publishing, a division of Periplus Editions (HK) Ltd.

The Tuttle Story: "Books to Span the East and West"

Many people are surprised to learn that the world's leading publisher of books on Asia had humble beginnings in the tiny American state of Vermont. The company's founder, Charles E. Tuttle, belonged to a New England family steeped in publishing.

Immediately after WWII, Tuttle served in Tokyo under General Douglas MacArthur and was tasked with reviving the Japanese publishing industry. He later founded the Charles E. Tuttle Publishing Company, which thrives today as one of the world's leading independent publishers.

Though a westerner, Tuttle was hugely instrumental in bringing a knowledge of Japan and Asia to a world hungry for information about the East. By the time of his death in 1993, Tuttle had published over 6,000 books on Asian culture, history and art—a legacy honored by the Japanese emperor with the "Order of the Sacred Treasure," the highest tribute Japan can bestow upon a non-Japanese.

With a backlist of 1,500 titles, Tuttle Publishing is more active today than at any time in its past— still inspired by Charles Tuttle's core mission to publish fine books to span the East and West and provide a greater understanding of each.

MAY 1 6 2017

ENOCH PRATT
WSH
FREE LIBRARY

WITHDRAWN FROM LIBRARY